בס"ד
לד' הארץ ומלואה

This book belongs to:

Please read it to me!

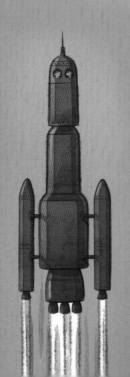

Hashem is Truly Everywhere

To my dear parents, Rabbi and Mrs. Kalmenson, for all their love and support. C.A.

To my dear parents, Gunter (Benjamin) and Linda (Esther) Lumer ע״ה
To my dear little Benny, my biggest fan and toughest critic. M.L.

Special thanks to master storyteller and educator, Rabbi Yosef Goldstein, "Uncle Yossi" who granted permission to the author of this book to use the classic verse he created: "Hashem is here, Hashem is there, Hashem it truly everywhere."

The word 'Hashem' is a respectful term that refers to G-d.

First Edition – Adar 5771 / March 2011
Second Impression – Elul 5772 / August 2012
Third Impression – Adar 1 5774 / February 2014.
Forth Impression – Nissan 5775 / April 2015

Editor: D.L. Rosenfeld
Managing Editor: Yossi Leverton

 Layout: MarcLumerDesign.com

ISBN: 978-1-929628-57-5
LCCN: 2010919501

HACHAI PUBLISHING
Brooklyn, New York
Tel: 718-633-0100 • Fax: 718-633-0103
www.hachai.com • info@hachai.com

The text of this book is set in Sunnydale.
The illustrations are in watercolor and pencil, touched up in Photoshop.

Printed in China

Hashem is Truly Everywhere

Story by Chani Altein
Artwork by Marc Lumer

Hachai
PUBLISHING

Tell me, tell me,
my friend Tzvi,
Do you know where
Hashem might be?

Is He right here on this spot?
Is He here with us, or not?

Yes! Hashem is on this spot.
There is no place where He is not!

Hashem is here, Hashem is there,
Hashem is truly everywhere.

Is He high up in the sky,
Where birds and planes go flying by?

There's no doubt Hashem is there,
Hashem is truly everywhere.

Is He with me in the night,
When I'm in bed, and there's no Light?

And is Hashem with me all day,
In school and out, through work and play?
Yes, He's with you every day,
In school and out, through work and play.

And He's with you in the night,
When you're in bed, and there's no Light.
Light and dark, here and there,
Hashem is truly everywhere.

Well,
what if
I go
far away?

What if
my trip
takes me
all day?

Doesn't matter — near or far,
Hashem is with you where you are.

Hashem is really every place,
Of course He's out in outer space!
I've told you many times before,
But I will tell you one time more:

High and low, dark and light,
Near and far, day and night,
In and out, here and there,
Hashem is truly everywhere!

Hashem is high up in the sky,
Where birds and planes go flying by.

Hashem is deep down in the sea,
Where only fishes seem to be.

Hashem is with me in the night,
When I'm in bed, and there's no light!

Hashem is with me every day,
In school and out, through work and play.

And even if I travel far,
By plane or train or boat or car,
Or rocket ship to outer space,

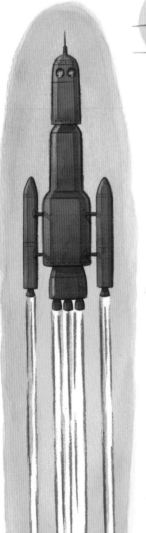

Hashem is really every place!

Exactly right! I'm glad to see
you understand so perfectly.

Hashem is here, Hashem is there,
Hashem is truly everywhere!